Cordelia, Dance!

STORY AND PICTURES BY

SARAH STAPLER

Dial Books for Young Readers New York

Published by Dial Books for Young Readers
A Division of Penguin Books USA Inc.
375 Hudson Street, New York, New York 10014

Design by Amelia Lau Carling
Printed in Hong Kong by South China Printing Company (1988) Limited
First Edition
W
1 3 5 7 9 10 8 6 4 2

Library of Congress Cataloging in Publication Data
Stapler, Sarah.
Cordelia, dance! / by Sarah Stapler.
p.   cm.
Summary: Cordelia the crocodile unhappily creates chaos in her
dance class, until she meets a student even clumsier than she is.
ISBN 0-8037-0792-4—ISBN 0-8037-0793-2 (lib. bdg.)
[1. Dancing—Fiction. 2. Clumsiness—Fiction.
3. Crocodiles—Fiction.] I. Title
PZ7.S7934Co 1990 [E]—dc20 89-39352 CIP AC

The art for each picture was created using pen-and-ink
and watercolor on bristol board. It was then color-separated and
reproduced in full-color.

For Meg and Sean
S.S.

Cordelia heard her mom's heavy footsteps as she strode into the room. "Cordelia, I have a surprise for you," she said. "You're going to dancing school and your first lesson is this week."

"Hurray!" Cordelia cried, nearly knocking over a train.

At the department store Cordelia and her mother looked at dresses for Cordelia. She tried on hundreds of them before she found the perfect one. When Cordelia looked in the mirror she knew that the red striped dress with the red heart pinafore was just right.

Cordelia was so excited when she arrived at the dancing school. Her mother introduced her to Miss Barker, the dancing school teacher. Then she said, "Have a wonderful evening."

But Cordelia did not have a wonderful evening.
During the first dance she stepped on Edgar's toes.
Then, practicing the rumba, she fell on Priscilla
and squished her flat.

The next dance Cordelia was so busy listening to
Miss Barker that she tripped up Alice with her tail
and accidentally hit Jane with her nose. "You clumsy
croc!" Jane wailed.

Finally Miss Barker asked Cordelia to *please* be more careful, because if she wasn't more careful she would be the only one left dancing.

Cordelia was so embarrassed.

Unfortunately when Cordelia sat down her tail caught in the chair, and when she stood up the chair went with her. By the fifth dance all the other dancers were talking about how clumsy she was.

"Look at her feet. They're like gunboats!"

"She hit Jane with that big nose of hers!"

"I wouldn't get in the way of that tail."

By the end no one wanted to dance with Cordelia.

The next dancing school evening Cordelia pretended to be sick. She told her mother that she had a stomachache. Her mother did not believe her.

That evening Miss Barker made the boys draw
their dancing partners' names from a hat to make
sure everyone danced.

Timothy fainted on the spot.

James disappeared before he could take Timothy's place.

And Peter refused to dance with her at all.

"Cordelia, why aren't you dressed for dancing?" her mom asked, one week later.

"Too much homework," Cordelia lied.

But it was Friday. "You'll have plenty of time to finish over the weekend," said her mom.

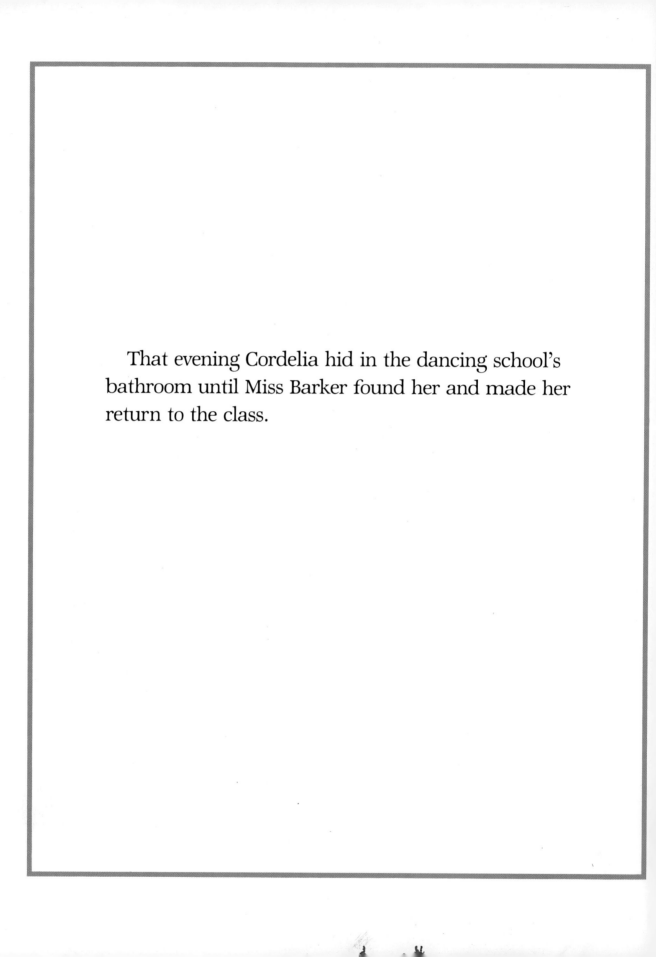

That evening Cordelia hid in the dancing school's bathroom until Miss Barker found her and made her return to the class.

The next dancing school evening Cordelia thought about running away, but decided to hide in her closet instead. Her mother was not amused.

That evening Cordelia was so late that she arrived at
the dancing school halfway through the lesson. She sat
and watched her classmates dance the rumba, then the
fox-trot, then the cha-cha-cha. Then they all waltzed.

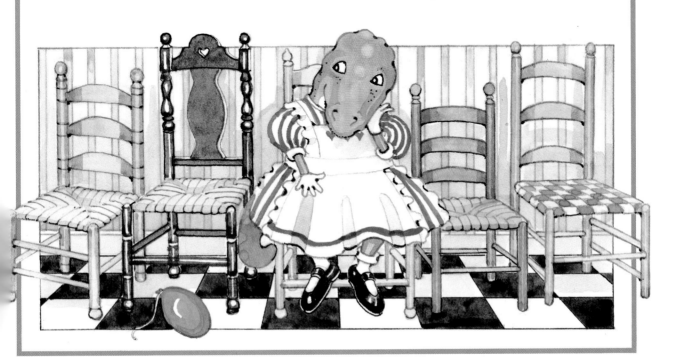

In the middle of the waltz Cordelia caught sight of
a figure sitting across the room. He was as green as
Cordelia and he looked as miserable as Cordelia felt.

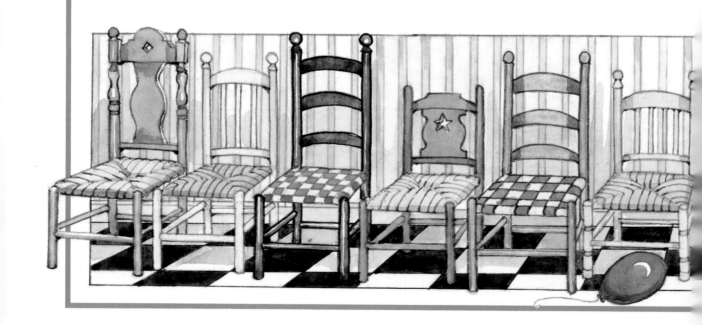

When Priscilla sat down she said, "His name is
Cornelius and he's even worse than you, Cordelia.
He cracked Jane's chair, stepped on Peter's foot,
and broke Miss Barker's pointer. Boy, was she mad!"

Cordelia knew just how he felt. She gathered all her courage and walked across the room to Cornelius. "Hi," she said in a tiny voice. Then Cordelia did a very brave thing. She asked Cornelius to dance.

Cordelia and Cornelius
attempted the cha-cha-cha,
tried the fox-trot, waltzed the rumba . . .

smashed the piano bench,
dented the wall,
stepped on Edgar's toes . . .

and had a wonderful time.